Dear Parent:

Congratulations! Your child is taking the first steps on an exciting journey. The destination? Independent reading!

STEP INTO READING® will help your child get there. The program offers books at five levels that accompany children from their first attempts at reading to reading success. Each step includes fun stories, fiction and nonfiction, and colorful art. There are also Step into Reading Sticker Books, Step into Reading Math Readers, and Step into Reading Phonics Readers— a complete literacy program with something to interest every child.

Learning to Read, Step by Step!

Ready to Read   Preschool–Kindergarten
• **big type and easy words** • **rhyme and rhythm** • **picture clues**
For children who know the alphabet and are eager to begin reading.

Reading with Help   Preschool–Grade 1
• **basic vocabulary** • **short sentences** • **simple stories**
For children who recognize familiar words and sound out new words with help.

Reading on Your Own   Grades 1–3
• **engaging characters** • **easy-to-follow plots** • **popular topics**
For children who are ready to read on their own.

Reading Paragraphs   Grades 2–3
• **challenging vocabulary** • **short paragraphs** • **exciting stories**
For newly independent readers who read simple sentences with confidence.

Ready for Chapters   Grades 2–4
• **chapters** • **longer paragraphs** • **full-color art**
For children who want to take the plunge into chapter books but still like colorful pictures.

STEP INTO READING® is designed to give every child a successful reading experience. The grade levels are only guides. Children can progress through the steps at their own speed, developing confidence in their reading, no matter what their grade.

Remember, a lifetime love of reading starts with a single step!

For the Glucklings, Alan and Max
—B.B.

For Liz, Bonnie, and Elise—dance troupe
of the imagination
—D.B.

www.stepintoreading.com

Educators and librarians, for a variety of teaching tools, visit us at
www.randomhouse.com/teachers

Library of Congress Cataloging-in-Publication Data
Bottner, Barbara.
Marsha is only a flower / by Barbara Bottner ; illustrated by Denise Brunkus.
   p.   cm. — (Step into reading. A step 3 book)
SUMMARY: All Lulu can think about is her solo role in her ballet recital, until she realizes that
she has hurt her younger sister.
ISBN 0-307-26330-4 (trade) — ISBN 0-307-46330-3 (lib. bdg.)
[1. Ballet—Fiction.   2. Sisters—Fiction.   3. Behavior—Fiction.]   I. Brunkus, Denise, ill.
II. Title.   III. Series: Step into reading. Step 3 book.
PZ7.B6586 Mai 2003 [E]—dc21   2002014816

Printed in the United States of America 14 13 12 11 10 9 8 7 6 5
First Random House Edition

Marsha Is Only a Flower

by Barbara Bottner
illustrated by Denise Brunkus

Random House 🏠 New York

"Look at me!

I'm a beautiful Princess," Lulu said.

She showed off her ballet costume

for Marsha.

"Someday, if you are lucky,

you might be a Princess, too.

But now you are only a Flower.

The littlest Flower in the whole show."

Lulu began to dance.
"I will show you the steps
for my solo," she said.
Lulu stood on her toes
and twirled.

Then she did a leap.

Marsha watched every step

Lulu made.

"Can you believe how well

I dance?" asked Lulu.

"Loo-loo," was all

Marsha could say.

"Now, show me

your Flower dance!" said Lulu.

Marsha wiggled on the floor.

Then she waved her arms.

"No! No! No!" yelled Lulu.

"Flowers don't wave!"

Marsha's head drooped.

She crawled away.

"Come back here!" cried Lulu.

But Marsha was gone.

Lulu sighed and got back to work.
It took hours and hours
of practice to be a Princess.
Tomorrow, at the ballet recital,
Marsha would see that Lulu
was truly a star.

11

Backstage the next morning,
Lulu put on her Princess costume.
"I want you to watch me
every single minute
I'm onstage,"
Lulu said to her mother.
"I will watch you and Marsha, too,"
her mother said.

"*Marsha!*

Why watch her?" asked Lulu.

"She is only a Flower."

But Lulu's mother didn't hear her.

She was too busy finding her seat.

Miss Miriam, the teacher,

brought the dancers together.

"Remember," she said,

"when I start to play,

Green Frog, Swan, and Evil Prince

leap onstage.

14

The Flowers will follow them.

Then it's Lulu's turn to do her solo.

Does everyone understand?"

They all nodded.

Even Marsha.

Then Miss Miriam went

to take her seat at the piano.

As soon as Miss Miriam

was out of sight,

Lulu said, "Don't forget.

Everyone came to see *me*.

The best dancer in the show."

"We are all good dancers," said Swan.

"Just as good as you!" said Green Frog.

"Maybe even better," said Evil Prince.

"You are not bad," said Lulu.

"But I'm the one with the solo."

Down in the pit, Miss Miriam
opened the sheet music.
"Ready? Here we go!"
she shouted.
She hit the first chords.

The blue lights turned purple.

The leaves fluttered.

"Everybody dance!" shouted Lulu.

"This is your cue!"

But nobody moved fast enough for Lulu.
So Lulu pushed Green Frog, Swan,
and Evil Prince onstage.
"It's your cue, too!" she said
to Marsha and the Flowers.
She pushed them onstage.

"Everybody dance together!"
Lulu shouted.

Soon it would be Lulu's turn.

Everyone was waiting for her solo.

And she was ready!

Finally, Miss Miriam played new chords.

Yes! It was time for the Princess.

"Scram, everybody!" Lulu shouted.
"It's my turn!"
Green Frog, Swan, Evil Prince,
and the Flowers danced
into the wings.

At last, Lulu jumped onstage.

The spotlight hit her eyes.

It was so bright!

How did her dance go?

Was it a twirl and then a leap?

Or a leap and then a twirl?

Lulu just stood there.

There were so many eyes
staring at her.
It was such a *big* stage,
she thought.
Nobody was on it.
Except for her.
Alone. All alone.

Miss Miriam played

the Princess song louder!

It was no use.

Lulu couldn't remember her steps.

What was she going to do?

Could she sing?

Could she juggle?

If only she could fly!

Suddenly, Lulu heard a sound.

Everyone was laughing.

Loudly.

Oh, no!

Were they laughing at her?

But then she saw that nobody
was even looking at her.
They were looking at *Marsha!*
They were laughing at *Marsha!*
The littlest Flower
had crawled back onstage.

Marsha grinned.

And giggled.

And waved.

Everyone loved Marsha!

For a minute Lulu
loved Marsha, too.

But the minute passed quickly.

"No wonder I can't dance!

You are in my way!"

Lulu hissed to Marsha.

Marsha's head drooped.

She crawled offstage.

Once again, the blue lights
turned purple.
The leaves fluttered.
Miss Miriam played the
Princess song again.
Now, Lulu remembered everything.

This time, she stood on her toes
and twirled and twirled.
She made giant leaps
across the stage.
Lulu was the most beautiful
Princess ever!
She never wanted to stop dancing.

But then Lulu saw something.

It was Marsha.

She was crawling toward
the edge of the stage.

She was in the wrong place
for a baby sister!

"Marsha, stop!" shouted Lulu.

But Marsha did not listen.

"Please!" begged Lulu.

But Marsha kept crawling.

"Help! Frog! Swan! Prince!"
called Lulu.
But Miss Miriam was playing
too loudly.
Nobody heard Lulu.

38

Lulu looked out at the audience.

Nobody even saw Marsha.

They were too busy looking at her.

No one was going to help

her baby sister.

Lulu would have to do it herself.

Lulu leaped over to Marsha.

She reached out to grab her.

At last, Green Frog, Swan,

and Evil Prince

saw what was happening.

They ran out to help.

Lulu picked Marsha up.

She twirled her around

as if it was part of her dance.

"Wheee!" giggled Marsha.

Marsha was safe!

But it was too late

for the others to stop.

They were running too fast.

They bumped right into

Lulu and Marsha.

Everyone rolled backstage

like a giant snowball.

The curtain dropped.

The audience shouted,
"Bravo! We want more!"
All the dancers crawled
out from under the curtain.
"They love us," said Green Frog.
"But everything went wrong!"
said Lulu.

Miss Miriam played an encore.

All the dancers bowed.

The audience stood up

and clapped even more.

Lulu beamed.

Backstage, Lulu's mother
hugged Marsha.
"My baby girl was in
her *first* recital!" she said.
Marsha smiled a silly smile.

"What about *me, me, me?*" asked Lulu.

"Lulu, you were wonderful!

In fact, both of you were wonderful!"

said her mother.

"Both of us?" asked Lulu.

"Both of you!" said her mother.

"Loo-loo!" Marsha said

as she waved her arms at Lulu.

Lulu looked over at her little sister.

"I decided that Princesses love Flowers,"
    said Lulu softly.

"Someday, it will be your turn
    to be a Princess.

And I am the perfect one
    to teach you."